CB036468

Anne of Green Gables

Anne arrives

L. M. Montgomery

About this Book

For the Student

🎧 Listen to the story and do some activities on your Audio CD
🎧 End of the listening excerpt
🗨 Talk about the story
tune• When you see the orange dot you can check the word in the glossary

K Prepare for Cambridge English: Key (KET) for Schools

For the Teacher

 A state-of-the-art interactive learning environment with 1000s of free online self-correcting activities for your chosen readers.

Go to our Readers Resource site for information on using readers and downloadable Resource Sheets, photocopiable Worksheets and Answer Keys. Plus free sample tracks from the story.

www.helblingreaders.com

For lots of great ideas on using Graded Readers consult Reading Matters, the Teacher's Guide to using Helbling Readers.

Level 2 Structures

Past simple of *be*	Comparative
Past simple	Comparative with *as...as*
Past simple (common irregular verbs)	Superlative
Be going to	*To* for purpose
Past continuous	Adverbs of manner
Past simple v. past continuous	
	A lot of, not much, not many
Past simple in questions	*And, so, but, because*
Have to / must	Possessive pronouns
Mustn't	

Structures from lower levels are also included

Contents

HELBLING DIGITAL

e·zone
THE EDUCATIONAL PLATFORM

**HELBLING e-zone
is an inspiring new
state-of-the-art, easy-to-use
interactive learning
environment.**

The online self-correcting
activities include:

- reading comprehension;
- listening comprehension;
- vocabulary;
- grammar;
- exam preparation.

■ **TEACHERS** register free of charge to set up classes and assign individual and class homework sets. Results are provided automatically once the deadline has been reached and detailed reports on performance are available at a click.

■ **STUDENTS** test their language skills in a stimulating interactive environment. All activities can be attempted as many times as necessary and full results and feedback are given as soon as the deadline has been reached. Single student access is also available.

FREE INTERACTIVE ONLINE TEACHING AND LEARNING MATERIALS

1000s of free online interactive activities now available for **HELBLING READERS** and your other favourite Helbling Languages publications.

www.
helbling-ezone.com
ONLINE ACTIVITIES

blog.helblingreaders.com

NEW

Love reading and readers and can't wait to get your class interested? Have a class library and reading programme but not sure how to take it a step further? The Helbling Readers BLOG is the place for you.

The **Helbling Readers BLOG** will provide you with ideas on setting up and running a Book Club and tips on reading lessons **every week**.

- Book Club
- Worksheets
- Lesson Plans

Subscribe to our **BLOG** and you will never miss out on our updates.

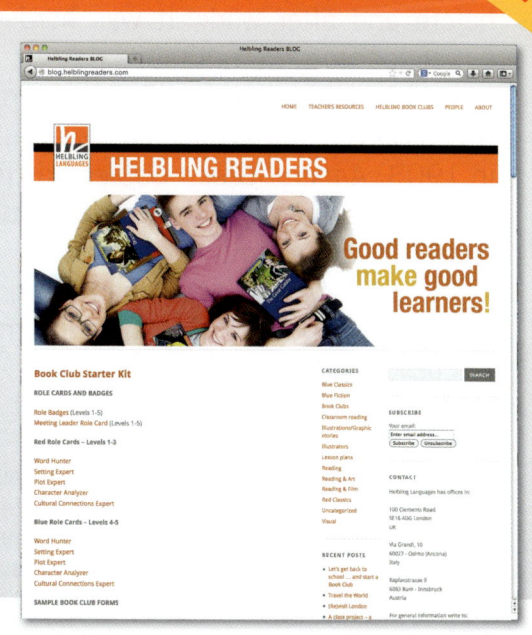

About the Author

Lucy Maud Montgomery was born in Clifton, Prince Edward Island in Canada in 1874. She was an only child*. Montgomery's mother died when she was 21 months old. Then she lived with her grandparents. They lived on a farm that was the inspiration* for 'Green Gables'.

Montgomery was an imaginative child. She liked boys' activities like fishing, climbing trees and inventing scary* ghost stories. In 1880 she started school. She already knew how to read and she started writing stories at nine years old. During her time at high school one of her poems was published.

In 1894 Montgomery went to university. She continued writing and in 1895 she published her first short story, for the fee* of five dollars.

After university she worked as a teacher but then she left to become a journalist for a newspaper. She also wrote her stories before and after work. It was hard work and she soon left the newspaper to write full time.

In 1904 Montgomery finished writing her first book, *Anne of Green Gables*. It was rejected* many times before it was published* in 1908. *Anne of Green Gables* was translated into 20 languages. Other books include: *Chronicles of Avonlea*, *Kilmeny of the Orchard*, and *Watchman and other poems*.

In 1911 Montgomery married a minister, Ewen Macdonald. They lived in Ontario (Canada) with their children.

Lucy Maud Montgomery died at the age of 68 in Toronto.

Glossary

- **fee:** price; money you earn
- **inspiration:** idea behind something
- **only child:** with no brothers or sisters
- **published:** put in a newspaper or book
- **rejected:** said 'no' to
- **scary:** that make you afraid

About the Book

***Anne of Green Gables** – Anne arrives* is set in Prince Edward Island in Canada in the late 1870s in a town called Avonlea. The novel follows the adventures of an 11-year-old orphan•, Anne. The main theme of the story is learning the difference between imagination and reality. Other themes are forgiveness• and vanity•.

The story begins when Anne is sent to Prince Edward Island after a difficult life of living in strangers' homes and orphanages•.

Matthew and Marilla Cuthbert decide to adopt• a boy from the orphanage to help Matthew on their farm. Through a misunderstanding, the orphanage sends a girl, Anne.

Anne talks a lot and is extremely imaginative. Marilla thinks Anne talks too much in the beginning. But Matthew loves her immediately. Although Marilla is disappointed that Anne is a girl, she takes pity on• her and decides to adopt her.

Anne promises to try to be good. She goes to the local school, finds a best friend, and has good times and bad times. It is her imagination that makes life interesting.

Montgomery's Anne is a much loved character in fiction and Mark Twain said Anne was 'the dearest and most moving• and delightful child since the immortal Alice' (from *Alice's Adventures in Wonderland*).

The TV film *Anne of Green Gables* (1985) won lots of awards and is a faithful adaptation of the book.

The next part of Anne's story continues in *Anne of Green Gables – Anne grows up*.

- **adopt:** take as their child
- **forgiveness:** when you accept that someone has made a mistake and you are not angry with them
- **moving:** that makes you feel good
- **orphan:** child with no living parents
- **orphanages:** places where children with no parents live
- **takes pity on:** feels sorry for
- **vanity:** obsessed with how you look

Before Reading

2 **1 Listen and match the descriptions to the characters. Number the pictures 1 to 6.**

Anne

Diana

Marilla

Gilbert

Mrs Rachel Lynde

Matthew

3 **2 Listen again and complete the sentences about the characters in Exercise 1.**

> handsome   round   black   red   older   long

1 Mrs Rachel Lynde had a .... face.

2 Anne had long .... hair.

3 Marilla had .... hair that she always wore in a bun.

4 Matthew was getting .... He was sixty.

5 Diana had black eyes and .... hair.

6 Gilbert was very .... He was almost fourteen.

3 **Look at the picture of Anne. Circle the adjectives that describe her.**

> plain clothes   grey eyes   red hair   freckles
> black hair   beautiful   blue eyes   plaits

4 **Now use the words in Exercise 3 to label the picture.**

5 **Work with a partner. Ask each other questions about Anne. Then ask and answer questions about each other.**

What does Anne look like?

What colour is your hair?

Anne is…

My hair is…

Before Reading

1 Match the words to the pictures.

> veranda   platform   house
> horse and buggy   kitchen   orphanage

....

....

2 Use the words from Exercise 1 to complete the sentences below.

a) There was a girl standing on the .... at the train station.

b) Green Gables was a big .... It was far from the main road.

c) The girl was living in an .... because she didn't have parents or relations.

d) They sat on the .... outside the house because it was cool.

e) They took the .... into town.

f) She set three plates on the table for supper in the ....

10

3 Look at the pictures and unscramble the words.

A HUCRCH

....

B NDRGAE

....

C OLOCSH

....

D WTNO

....

K 4 Read the descriptions of these places in the story. What is the word for each one? The first letter is already there. There is one space for each other letter in the word. Use the pictures to help you.

a) Children go here to learn things. **S** _ _ _ _ _

b) People often grow flowers and have grass here. **G** _ _ _ _ _

c) People go here every Sunday to pray. **C** _ _ _ _ _

d) A group of houses with shops and a church. **T** _ _ _

5 Use the words from Exercise 3 to complete the sentences below.

a) Mr Philips was the teacher at the ....

b) The woman was in the .... picking flowers.

c) The story is set in a small .... called Avonlea.

d) Marilla sent Anne to .... every Sunday.

1 Mrs Rachel Lynde is surprised

Mrs Rachel Lynde was a curious woman. She knew everything about Avonlea. Mrs Rachel lived in a part of Avonlea called Lynde's Hollow. She saw everyone coming into town and everyone going out. Mrs Rachel was more curious° than most people but she was also very helpful.

Today she was very curious about Matthew Cuthbert. Matthew was dressed in his best clothes and he was driving his horse and buggy° past her house.

'Where is Matthew Cuthbert going?' she asked out loud.

'I can go to Green Gables and ask Marilla,' she thought.

Marilla was Matthew's sister. Marilla and Matthew lived together at Green Gables. Green Gables was a big house. It was far from the main road.

Mrs Rachel knocked on the kitchen door and went into the house. The kitchen at Green Gables was a nice room but it was too tidy°. Marilla Cuthbert was in her chair knitting° and the table behind her was set° for supper. There were three plates on the table. Mrs Rachel was very confused.

'Good evening, Rachel,' Marilla said kindly. 'Come in and sit down. How is your family?'

Marilla was a tall, thin woman. She had dark hair that she always wore in a bun°. She looked like a severe woman but her mouth was soft. Maybe she laughed sometimes. The women were very different but they were friends.

Glossary

- **buggy:**
- **curious:** interested to know things
- **in a bun:**
- **knitting:**
- **set:** prepared
- **tidy:** very organized and clean

'We're all quite well,' said Mrs Rachel. 'But I thought that *you* weren't well because I saw Matthew leaving today. Was he going to the doctor's?'

Marilla replied patiently, 'Oh, no, we're quite well. Matthew went to Bright River. We're getting a little boy from an orphanage• in Nova Scotia and he's coming on the train tonight.'

Mrs Rachel was so shocked that she was unable to speak for five seconds.

'Are you serious, Marilla?' she asked.

'Yes, of course,' said Marilla, calmly.

'What put such an idea into your head?' asked Mrs Rachel disapprovingly•.

'Well, we thought about it for a long time. We thought all winter,' replied Marilla. 'A neighbor talked about getting a little girl from the orphanage in the spring. So Matthew and I decided to get a boy. Matthew is getting older, he's sixty. And he has heart problems. We asked for an intelligent boy of about ten or eleven. A boy old enough to do the chores• and young enough to be trained• properly. Then we got a telegram•: the young boy is coming on the five thirty train tonight. Matthew went to the train station at Bright River to meet him.'

NEWS
What news shocked Mrs Rachel? Why?

Glossary

- **chores:** jobs around the house
- **disapprovingly:** in a way that shows she doesn't agree
- **orphanage:** place where children without parents live
- **telegram:** printed message sent by the post office
- **trained:** taught to do things

'Well, Marilla, I think you're doing a very risky• thing. You're bringing a strange child into your home. You don't know anything about him. You don't know what he is like•, or what his parents were like.'

Marilla continued knitting.

'You are right, Rachel. I do worry, but Matthew is convinced•. There are risks in almost everything in this world. He can't be very different from us.'

'Well, I hope everything is okay,' said Mrs Rachel, doubtfully. 'I heard an orphan• girl put poison• in a well• and the whole family died.'

'We're not getting a girl,' said Marilla. 'I definitely don't want a girl.'

Mrs Rachel left because she wanted to tell the news to everyone she met on the way home.

'Well,' thought Mrs Rachel as she left Green Gables. 'I'm sorry for that poor boy. Matthew and Marilla don't know anything about children.'

But the child at the station was not what everyone expected•.

GUESS

Why do you think the child at the station is different?

- **convinced:** (here) sure; certain
- **expected:** was waiting for
- **orphan:** child with no living parents
- **poison:** substance that can kill you
- **risky:** dangerous
- **well:** deep hole in the ground for water
- **what he is like:** how he is physically and mentally

2 Matthew Cuthbert is surprised

Matthew Cuthbert and his horse traveled to Bright River Station. Matthew enjoyed being alone. He was afraid of most women except° Marilla and Mrs Rachel. Other women laughed at him because he looked strange.

At Bright River Station Matthew thought he was too early. There was no train. On the platform° there was a young girl waiting. Matthew did not come for a girl. He went to speak to the stationmaster°.

'The train arrived thirty minutes ago,' said the stationmaster. 'There is a passenger° for you. She's standing on the platform. She wanted to stay outside. She is strange.'

'I'm not here for a *girl*,' said Matthew. 'I came for a boy. He was coming from Nova Scotia.'

'Well, I don't know,' said the stationmaster. 'The girl is for you. I don't have any other orphans here for you.'

'I don't understand,' said Matthew.

'Well, ask the girl,' said the stationmaster. 'She can explain. She likes talking. Maybe they didn't have any boys to send today.'

Matthew felt very nervous. He was afraid of speaking to girls or women he didn't know.

The girl was about eleven. She was unusual° looking. She was wearing an ugly yellow dress and an old brown hat. And her long red hair was in two plaits. Matthew felt afraid.

'Are you Mr Matthew Cuthbert of Green Gables?' said the girl. 'It's very nice to meet you. I thought you weren't coming.'

Glossary

- **except:** but not
- **passenger:** person who travels in a car, train but doesn't drive it
- **platform:** place where you wait for a train
- **stationmaster:** person responsible at a train station
- **unusual:** strange; not normal

BRIGHT RIVER

'I'm sorry I was late,' said Matthew. 'Come. The horse is over there. Give me your bag.'

'Oh, I can carry it,' the girl said happily. 'Oh, I'm very glad• you're here. Oh, it is so wonderful. I'm going to belong to you•. I didn't belong to anybody in the past. I was at the orphanage for four months. An orphanage is a terrible place. It's worse than anything you can imagine.'

Matthew decided not to tell the girl there was a mistake•. Marilla was good at these situations.

Matthew and Anne got into the buggy. They drove out of the village. Then the girl started talking again.

'I love pretty clothes. I don't have a pretty dress. Can I have a pretty dress? Oh, dear! Am I talking too much? People always tell me I that I talk too much. Do you want me to stop talking? I *can* stop when I decide. But it *is* difficult.'

Matthew felt good, surprisingly. He did not expect to enjoy Anne's company. But this girl was very different. He liked listening to her. So he said shyly•:

'Oh, talk as much as you like. I don't mind•.'

The girl continued, 'Oh, I'm so glad. I know you and I are going to be good friends. I do like talking. I don't like being told to be quiet. People tell me to be quiet all the time.'

And she continued talking, and talked nearly all the way to Green Gables.

Glossary

- **belong to you:** (here) become part of your family
- **glad:** happy
- **I don't mind:** it's okay for me
- **mistake:** error; wrong thing
- **shyly:** in a quiet unsure way

TALKING

Do you like talking?
Do you think some
people talk too much?

'That's Green Gables over…' said Matthew.

'Oh, don't tell me,' said the girl. Her eyes were shut. 'I want to guess. I'm sure I can guess right.'

She opened her eyes. They were on the top of a hill. She saw a star over a house. 'That's it, isn't it?' she said, pointing to Green Gables.

'You guessed it!' said Matthew. The horse started moving again.

'I felt it was home immediately. Oh, I can't believe this is true.'

They arrived at Green Gables. Matthew was feeling very bad. He was not worried about Marilla. He was very worried about disappointing this young girl.

The girl followed Matthew into the house. Marilla was waiting to meet an orphan boy.

3 Marilla Cuthbert is surprised

Matthew opened the door. The person with him shocked Marilla.

'Matthew Cuthbert, who is that? Where is the boy?' said Marilla angrily.

'There was no *boy*,' said Matthew sadly. 'There was only this *girl*.'

'No boy! But there must be a boy,' said Marilla. 'We asked Mrs Spencer for a boy.'

'Well, she gave us a girl. There is definitely a mistake. But I had to bring the girl home. It's not right to leave a girl at the station.'

'Well, this is a terrible situation,' said Marilla.

The girl was silent.

'You don't want me,' she said suddenly. 'You don't want me because I'm not a boy. I knew it. Nobody wants me. Oh, I'm going to cry.'

The girl started crying. Then she sat down and cried harder•. Marilla and Matthew didn't know what to say or do.

'There's no need to cry about it,' said Marilla.

'Yes, there is,' said the girl, crying. 'I thought I had a home. Then you say you don't want me because I'm not a boy. Oh, this is terrible.'

> # GIRL
> Imagine you are the girl.
> How do you feel?

Glossary

• **harder:** (here) more and louder

Marilla felt her heart soften•.

'Well, don't cry now. We're not going to send you back tonight. We can investigate• tomorrow. What's your name?'

'Can you please call me Cordelia?' asked the girl.

'Is that your name?' asked Marilla.

'No, it's not. But I love the name Cordelia. It's such an elegant name.'

'What is your real name?' asked Marilla.

'Anne Shirley,' said the girl slowly, 'But, please call me Cordelia. I'm not going to be here long. And Anne is such an unromantic name.'

'Unromantic, nonsense•!' said Marilla. 'Anne is a sensible• name.'

'Can you please remember to call me Anne spelled with an E ?'

'What difference does it make how it's spelled?' asked Marilla.

'Oh, it makes a big difference. It looks much nicer.'

> # NAME
> How do you spell your name?
> Can you spell your name in another way?
> What other names do you like?
> Can you imagine having another name?

Glossary

- **investigate:** find out
- **nonsense:** something stupid
- **sensible:** practical
- **soften:** become tender and kind

'Okay, Anne spelled with an E. Why are you here? We asked for a boy. Were there no boys at the orphanage? We want a boy to help Matthew on the farm. A girl is useless,' said Marilla.

'Oh, yes, there were lots of boys. But Mrs Spencer definitely told the orphanage that you wanted a girl. A girl around eleven years old. I was so happy that I didn't sleep last night.'

Anne turned to Matthew.

'Oh, why didn't you tell me at the station that you didn't want me', she said. 'Why didn't you leave me there?'

'I'm going to put the horse in•, Marilla,' said Matthew quickly. 'Have dinner ready when I get back.'

Later they all sat down to eat dinner. But Anne could not eat.

'I can't eat' she said. 'I'm in the depths of despair•. How can you eat when you are in the depths of despair?'

'I don't get that sad,' said Marilla.

'Well, can't you try to imagine you are in the depths of despair?'

'No, I can't.'

'Well, you can't understand it. It's a very uncomfortable feeling. You can't swallow. You can't even eat chocolate. I do hope you're not offended• because I can't eat.'

'I think she's tired,' said Matthew. 'It is best that Anne goes to bed, Marilla.'

Glossary

- **in the depths of despair:** feeling very sad
- **offended:** hurt; sad
- **to put the horse in:** take the horse to the stable

After putting Anne to bed, Marilla went to the kitchen to wash the dishes. Matthew was smoking his pipe•.

'Well, this is a disaster,' she said angrily. 'I must see Mrs Spencer tomorrow. This girl must go back to the orphanage.'

'Yes, I suppose so,' said Matthew.

'You *suppose* so. Don't you agree?'

'Well, she's a nice girl, Marilla. It's a pity• to send her back. She really wants to stay.'

'No! What can she do for us?'

'We can do something for her,' said Matthew.

'Matthew Cuthbert, I believe that child has charmed• you. You want to keep• her.'

'She's a really interesting girl,' said Matthew. 'The way she talks.'

'Oh, she can talk. I heard that immediately. Talking is *not* a good thing. No, she has to go back immediately.'

'I can hire• a French boy to help me,' said Matthew, 'and Anne can be company for you.'

'I don't need more company,' said Marilla. 'And I'm not going to keep her.'

'Of course, Marilla,' said Matthew. He put his pipe away. 'I'm going to bed.'

Marilla finished putting the dishes away. She went to bed unhappily.

Upstairs Anne cried herself to sleep.

- **charmed:** fascinated; made you like her
- **hire:** employ; give a job to
- **keep:** have; (here) adopt

- **pipe:**
- **pity:** not fortunate; sad

When Anne woke up she didn't know where she was. Suddenly she remembered. This was Green Gables. Marilla and Matthew didn't want her because she wasn't a boy.

But it was a beautiful morning. Anne looked out the window. Green Gables was lovely. But she wasn't going to stay here.

Suddenly Marilla interrupted Anne's daydream•.

'Get dressed, Anne,' said Marilla.

Marilla didn't know how to talk to children.

'Oh, isn't it wonderful?' said Anne.

'What? The cherry tree?' asked Marilla, 'It has nice flowers. But the cherries aren't very good.'

'Oh, I don't mean only the tree. I meant everything. You think it doesn't make a difference because you're not going to keep me. But I want to remember everything. I'm not in the depths of despair this morning. But I feel very sad.'

'Get dressed and stop feeling sad,' said Marilla. 'Breakfast is waiting. Make your bed. Be quick.'

Anne was very quick. She did almost everything in ten minutes. But she forgot about the bed.

'I'm quite hungry this morning,' said Anne. 'The world doesn't seem such a dark place now. I'm so glad it's sunny. I like rainy mornings, too. But difficult situations are easier on a sunny day.'

'Oh, be quiet,' said Marilla. 'You talk too much.'

WEATHER
Are you happier on sunny or rainy days?
What weather do you like best?
Tell a friend.

During breakfast, Anne acted strangely. She ate mechanically•. She was staring• out the window. What person wants a girl like this in their home?

But Matthew wanted to keep her. Marilla understood Matthew's silent persistence•.

When the meal ended Anne offered to wash the dishes.

Anne washed the dishes quickly. Marilla watched carefully. Later Anne made her bed less successfully. She didn't know how to make a bed.

Marilla then told Anne to play outside until lunch. 'After lunch we are going to see Mrs Spencer to resolve• the situation,' Marilla explained.

Anne ran to the door. Suddenly she stopped and sat down. She was very sad.

'What's wrong now?' demanded Marilla.

'I don't want to go out,' said Anne, 'I can't stay here. I don't want to see Green Gables. I don't want to love things. Then I have to leave them. I don't think I can go out. What is the name of that geranium• by the window, please?'

'That's an apple-scented• geranium.'

'Oh, I don't mean that sort of name. Didn't you give it a name? Can I call it Bonny? That's a nice name. Can I call it Bonny for now?'

'Goodness, I don't care•. Geraniums don't have names.'

'Oh, I like all things to have names. It makes them seem more like people. Imagine being called "a geranium". You can't be happy just being called "woman".'

Glossary

- **apple-scented:** it smells like apples
- **daydream:** things she imagined/ dreamed while awake
- **don't care:** am not interested
- **geranium:** type of flower
- **mechanically:** like a robot
- **persistence:** determination
- **resolve:** fix
- **staring:** looking for a long time

'She's unusual,' thought Marilla. 'And Matthew's right: she's interesting. She has charmed Matthew and now she's charming me.'

Marilla made lunch. They ate and then she asked Matthew to get the horse and buggy ready.

'I'm going to see Mrs Spencer to resolve this,' said Marilla. 'I'm taking Anne with me.'

Matthew was silent.

As Marilla and Anne were leaving Matthew said:

'Jerry Buote was here this morning. I'm going to hire him for the summer.'

Marilla was silent. She hit the horse hard and made it gallop. Matthew watched Marilla and Anne leave.

5 Anne's history

'I'm going to enjoy this drive,' Anne said. 'Oh, look, there's a wild rose. Pink is a wonderful color. But redheaded people can't wear pink. Do you think red hair can change color?'

'No, I don't,' said Marilla. 'Now, I know you like talking, so tell me about your life.'

'Oh, what I *know* about me isn't very interesting,' said Anne. 'I can tell you what I *imagine*.'

'No, I just want the facts,' said Marilla. 'Begin at the beginning. Where were you born and how old are you?'

'I was eleven last March,' said Anne. 'And I was born in Bolingbroke, Nova Scotia. My father's name was Walter Shirley. He was a teacher. My mother's name was Bertha Shirley. I'm so glad my parents had nice names. My mother was a teacher before she married my father. They were poor. I was three months old when my mother died. And my father died four days later. That left me an orphan. Nobody wanted me. Father and mother didn't have relatives•.'

RELATIVES
Have YOU got any relatives?
Write a list.

• **relatives:** people connected to your family by birth or marriage

'Then Mrs Thomas took me,' Anne continued. 'She was poor and she had a drunken• husband. Mrs Thomas was very strict•. I was naughty• sometimes but she was fair•.' I lived with them until I was eight years old. I helped look after her four children. Then Mr Thomas died. His mother offered to take Mrs Thomas and the children but not me. Then Mrs Hammond took me because she knew I was good with children. She had eight children. She had twins three times. I like babies, but twins three times is *too much*. I lived with Mrs Hammond for about two years. Then Mr Hammond died and Mrs Hammond went to the USA•. I went to the orphanage at Hopeton. I was there four months until Mrs Spencer came.'

Anne finished her story. She didn't like talking about her life.

'Did you go to school?' asked Marilla.

'I went for a year. I didn't go to school when I lived with Mrs Hammond. But I went at the orphanage. I can read quite well. I can remember lots of poetry.'

'Were Mrs Thomas and Mrs Hammond good to you?' asked Marilla.

'Oh,' said Anne. 'People want to be good to you. But they had a lot to worry about. Bad husbands and lots of children.'

Marilla asked no more questions. She suddenly thought Matthew's idea to keep Anne was not impossible.

- **drunken:** person who drinks too much alcohol
- **fair:** did the right thing
- **naughty:** bad (usually of a child)
- **strict:** severe
- **the USA:** the United States of America

'She talks too much,' thought Marilla, 'but I can train her. She's ladylike. Her parents were probably nice.'

'Oh, what big house is that, please?' said Anne.

'It's a hotel,' Marilla replied.

'I was afraid that it was Mrs Spencer's house,' said Anne. 'I don't want to arrive there.'

6 Marilla decides

Marilla and Anne arrived at Mrs Spencer's house.

'I didn't expect to see you two today. How are you, Anne?'

'I'm okay, thank you,' said Anne. She didn't smile.

'Do you want some tea, Marilla?' asked Mrs Spencer.

'Yes,' said Marilla. 'But I can't stay long. You see, Mrs Spencer, someone made a mistake. We sent a message through your brother that we wanted a boy. A ten- or eleven-year-old boy.'

'Oh no!' said Mrs Spencer. 'My brother told his daughter Nancy. Then Nancy told us that you wanted a girl. I'm so sorry.'

'It was our fault•,' said Marilla. 'Now let's make it right. Can we send the child back to the orphanage?'

'I suppose so,' said Mrs Spencer, thoughtfully, 'but we don't need to send her back. Mrs Blewett was here yesterday. She said that she wanted a little girl. Anne is perfect for her.'

Marilla knew about Mrs Blewett. She was a mean• employer. Her children were difficult, too. Marilla felt bad about sending Anne to this woman.

'Well, let's talk about it,' said Marilla.

'Oh, look! Here comes Mrs Blewett,' said Mrs Spencer. 'Good afternoon, Mrs Blewett. Let me introduce you. Mrs Blewett this is Miss Cuthbert.'

Anne stared at Mrs Blewett. The woman looked mean.

'It seems there was a mistake, Mrs Blewett. I thought that Mr and Miss Cuthbert wanted a girl. But they wanted a boy. I think this girl is perfect for you.'

Mrs Blewett looked at Anne.

- **fault:** responsibility
- **mean:** really unkind

'How old are you and what's your name?' Mrs Blewett asked.

'Anne Shirley,' said Anne, 'and I'm eleven years old.' She did not talk about the spelling of her name.

'Well, you don't look very strong. You have to be smart• and respectful• at my house. I expect you to work. Yes, I can take her now, Miss Cuthbert.'

Marilla looked at Anne. Anne looked scared. Marilla was *not* going to give Anne to Mrs Blewett. She did not trust this woman.

'Well, I don't know,' said Marilla. 'I think Matthew wants to keep Anne. I want to take her home again and talk to Matthew. Is that okay, Mrs Blewett?'

'I suppose it is,' said Mrs Blewett.

Mrs Spencer and Mrs Blewett left the room. Anne was relieved•. Suddenly she ran to Marilla.

'Oh, Miss Cuthbert, did you really say that I can stay at Green Gables?' she whispered•. 'Or did I only imagine it?'

'Yes, I said that,' said Marilla. 'It isn't decided. Mrs Blewett needs you more than I do.'

'I want to go back to the orphanage. I can't live with her,' said Anne. 'She looks very mean.'

Marilla tried not to smile.

'A little girl can't talk about a lady like that,' said Marilla. 'Go and sit quietly. Be a good girl.'

'I can try to be anything you want. I want you to keep me,' said Anne. And she sat down again.

Glossary

- **relieved:** full of thanks; happy
- **respectful:** when you are good and considerate to another person
- **smart:** (here) tidy and clean
- **whispered:** spoke in a low voice

Later that evening, Matthew came out to meet Anne and Marilla when they arrived at Green Gables. He was happy to see them both. Marilla put Anne to bed. Then she told Matthew about Anne's history. She also told him about Mrs Blewett.

'Mrs Blewett is a mean woman,' said Matthew.

'I don't like her, either,' said Marilla. 'I was thinking about keeping Anne. I don't know much about children, but I can do my best. She can stay.'

Matthew was delighted•.

'I am so glad, Marilla,' he said. 'She's an interesting child.'

'A useful child is better,' said Marilla, 'but I can train her to be useful. And, Matthew, you can't interfere•. Perhaps I don't know much about raising• a child. But I know more than you.'

'Of course, Marilla,' said Matthew. 'Be kind without spoiling• her. I think love is the key.'

Marilla decided to tell Anne the news the next day.

RAISING A CHILD
What does Marilla say about raising a child?
What does Matthew say about raising a child?
What do YOU think about raising a child?
Discuss with a friend.

Glossary

- **delighted:** very happy
- **interfere:** get involved
- **raising:** helping someone grow
- **spoiling:** making someone bad by being too indulgent

7 Raising Anne

The next day Anne finished washing the lunch dishes. She turned to Marilla.

'Oh, please, Miss Cuthbert, can I stay? I really need to know. Please tell me.'

'Well,' said Marilla, 'Yes, you can stay. You must try to be a good girl. What's wrong•?'

'Oh, I'm so happy,' said Anne with tears in her eyes.

'Maybe you're very excited,' said Marilla. 'Matthew and I promise to try to be good to you. You must go to school. But in two weeks school stops for the summer. So you can start in September.'

'What can I call you?' asked Anne. 'Can I call you Aunt Marilla?'

'No, just call me Marilla.'

' "Marilla" doesn't sound polite•,' replied Anne.

'Everyone calls me Marilla.'

'I really want to call you Aunt Marilla,' said Anne thoughtfully. 'I haven't got any aunts. Can't I call you Aunt Marilla? We can imagine you are my aunt.'

'No,' said Marilla firmly•.

'Do you never imagine things?' asked Anne.

'No.'

'Oh, Marilla! That's sad!'

- **firmly:** in a sure, decided way
- **polite:** (here) appropriate; the correct thing
- **what's wrong:** is there a problem

'Marilla, do you think that I can have a best friend in Avonlea?'

'What kind of friend?'

'A best friend. A very close friend. I dream of meeting her. I can tell all my secrets to her.'

'Diana Barry lives near. She's the same age as you. Maybe she can be your friend. She's not home now, but when she comes back you can meet her. Her mother, Mrs Barry, is a very unusual woman. She doesn't allow Diana to play with bad girls. You have to be careful how you behave•.'

'What is Diana like? I hope she doesn't have red hair.'

'Diana is a pretty girl. She has black eyes and black hair. And she is good and smart•. That's better than being pretty.'

Marilla liked morals•. She thought that a moral was always necessary.

But Anne didn't hear the moral. She was interested in her new 'friend'.

'Oh, I'm so glad she's pretty. I can't be beautiful so a beautiful best friend is wonderful.'

BEST FRIEND

Do you have a best friend?
What is he/she like?
Describe him/her to the class.
Remember to include:
- hair
- eyes
- character

Glossary

- **behave:** act
- **freckles:** small brown spots of color on your skin
- **morals:** life lessons
- **smart:** (here) intelligent

'At Mrs Thomas' house,' Anne continued. 'I had an imaginary friend. I called her Katie Maurice. I told her everything. Then I went to live with Mrs Hammond and I had another imaginary friend. Her name was Violetta. We were great friends.'

'You need a real friend. And don't talk about your imaginary friend with Mrs Barry,' said Marilla. 'Now go to your room.'

Anne went to her room and sat down in a chair by the window. Then she began daydreaming again. She looked at her face in the mirror. Anne saw freckles• and grey eyes.

'You're Anne of Green Gables,' she said and she kissed the mirror.

Then she went to the window and opened it.

'Dear trees, good afternoon,' Anne said out of the window. 'I hope pretty Diana is going to be my best friend. But I must never forget Katie Maurice and Violetta.'

Anne blew kisses to her imaginary friends.

8 Mrs Rachel is shocked

After two weeks Mrs Rachel Lynde went to visit Marilla.

'I heard there was a mistake with the orphan child,' said Mrs Rachel. 'Did you not want to send her back?'

'We decided not to. Matthew likes her. And I like her, too. The house seems different already. She's a bright• child.'

'You have a big responsibility,' said Mrs Rachel. 'You don't have any experience with children. You don't know much about her. But I don't want to discourage• you, Marilla.'

'I'm not discouraged,' said Marilla, 'I decided. And that's all. Do you want to meet Anne?'

Anne ran inside happily. She stopped suddenly when she saw the stranger•.

Mrs Rachel studied Anne. Anne's clothes were very strange. There were lots of freckles on her face. And her hair was very red.

'Well, you're not pretty,' Mrs Rachel said.

Mrs Rachel always said what she thought.

'You're very skinny• and plain•. Come here, I want to look at you. Look at your freckles. And your hair is as red as carrots.'

Anne stared at Mrs Rachel. Anne's face became redder than her hair!

'I hate you,' screamed• Anne. 'I hate you! I hate you! I hate you! How dare you• call me skinny and plain! How dare you say I'm freckled and redheaded! You are a very rude• woman.'

Glossary

- **bright:** intelligent
- **dare you:** can you have the courage to
- **discourage:** convince someone not to do something
- **plain:** not pretty
- **rude:** not polite and not respectful
- **screamed:** shouted loudly and angrily
- **skinny:** very thin
- **stranger:** someone you don't know

RUDE

How is Mrs Rachel rude?
How is Anne rude?

'Anne!' said Marilla.

But Anne stared angrily at Mrs Rachel.

'You are fat,' said Anne. 'You probably don't have any imagination. I don't care about insulting• you. You insulted me. And I can't *ever•* forgive you.'

'What a temper•!' said Mrs Rachel. She was horrified.

'Anne, go to your room. Stay there until I come up,' said Marilla. She was very shocked.

Anne ran to the door and slammed• it hard. She ran to her room and slammed that door, too.

'There's a lot of work in raising *that* child, Marilla,' said Mrs Rachel.

Marilla didn't know what to say.

'The things you said were mean, Rachel.'

'Marilla Cuthbert, are you defending Anne's bad behavior•?' asked Mrs Rachel.

'No,' said Marilla, 'She was very naughty. She must be punished•. But she doesn't know how to be polite. And you *were* mean to her, Rachel.'

Marilla had to say that last sentence. But she was surprised she did.

Mrs Rachel stood. She was offended.

'Well, I feel sorry for you, Marilla. That child is trouble. My advice is to beat• her. Children listen when you beat them. But I suppose you aren't going to listen to me. Good evening, Marilla. Come to see me often as usual. But I can't visit here again. I can't be insulted like that again.'

Then Mrs Rachel left Green Gables quickly.

Glossary

- **beat:** hit
- **behavior:** way you act
- **ever:** at any time
- **insulting:** offending
- **punished:** disciplined
- **slammed:** shut with great force
- **temper:** angry state of mind

> Who do YOU agree with? Tick (✓).
> ☐ Anne
> ☐ Mrs Rachel
> ☐ Marilla

Marilla went to Anne's bedroom.

On the way she thought about Anne's punishment•. Marilla didn't agree with beating children. She was more worried that Mrs Rachel saw Anne's temper. Mrs Rachel liked to gossip•.

Marilla found Anne crying on her bed.

'Anne, aren't you ashamed of• your behavior?' asked Marilla.

'She was mean calling me plain and redheaded,' cried Anne.

'You were mean, too. And your behavior disgraced me•. You often say you have red hair. You complain• about not being pretty.'

'Oh, but it's different with me saying it,' said Anne. 'She said terrible things. I had to say something.'

'Well, now Mrs Rachel has a terrible story to tell everyone.'

'Imagine someone said that you were plain,' said Anne.

Suddenly Marilla remembered something from her childhood•. She remembered when someone said to her that she was very plain. Marilla remembered that she was sad for a long time after that comment.

EMPATHY
Can you remember something like this from your childhood? Does this help you understand how Anne feels?

- **ashamed of:** embarrassed about
- **childhood:** when you are a child
- **complain:** talk a lot about things you don't like
- **disgraced me:** made me look bad
- **gossip:** talking about someone when they aren't there
- **punishment:** penalty for doing something bad

'I didn't say that Mrs Rachel's words were okay,' said Marilla. Her voice was friendly now. 'But you were rude. She is an elderly° person and my visitor. You must be respectful.'

Suddenly Marilla had an idea.

'You must go to Mrs Rachel and apologize°.'

'I can't do that,' said Anne. 'You can put me in a prison° with snakes. But I cannot ask Mrs Rachel to forgive me.'

'We don't put people in prisons here, Anne,' said Marilla. 'But you must apologize to Mrs Rachel. You must stay in your room until you're ready to apologize.'

'I have to stay here forever° then,' said Anne sadly. 'I can't apologize to Mrs Rachel. I'm *not* sorry. I'm sorry I disgraced you. But I'm glad I told her what I think. I can't even imagine I'm sorry.'

'Perhaps you can imagine better in the morning,' said Marilla. 'Think about your behavior tonight. You promised to try to be very good while you are at Green Gables. This is not a good start.'

Marilla went to the kitchen. She was very angry but she also felt like laughing. She remembered Mrs Rachel's face as Anne told her the truth. Marilla started to laugh.

Glossary

- **apologize:** say you're sorry
- **elderly:** old
- **forever:** always; from now on
- **humiliating:** embarrassing
- **prison:** locked building for criminals

9 Anne's apology

The next morning Marilla told Matthew about Anne's behavior.

'Rachel Lynde is a terrible gossip. I think Anne did a good thing' said Matthew.

'Matthew Cuthbert! I suppose you think that no punishment is necessary?'

'Well, I think a little punishment is necessary,' said Matthew. 'Remember nobody ever taught her before.'

'She stays in her room until she's ready to apologize to Mrs Rachel. That's final, Matthew,' said Marilla.

Breakfast, dinner and supper were very silent meals. Anne stayed in her room.

Matthew waited for Marilla to go outside. Secretly he went to Anne's room.

Anne was by the window. She looked unhappy. Matthew felt sad.

Matthew spoke quickly. He didn't want Marilla to hear him.

'Anne, how about doing it? Then you can eat with us again,' he whispered.

'Do you mean "apologize" to Mrs Rachel?'

'Yes. Apologize. That's the word,' said Matthew. 'Say it.'

'I can do it for you,' said Anne. 'I am sorry now. I wasn't sorry last night. But this morning I felt so ashamed. But I didn't want to tell Mrs Rachel. It is so humiliating•. But do you want me to do it for you?'

'Yes, I do. It's very lonely without you.'

'Okay,' said Anne. 'I'm ready to apologize.'

'Good, Anne. But don't tell Marilla I spoke to you.'

'I promise,' said Anne.

Matthew left quickly.

Later Marilla was happily surprised by Anne's words.

'I'm sorry I was rude yesterday,' said Anne. 'I'm ready to apologize to Mrs Rachel.'

On the way to Mrs Rachel's house Anne's mood• changed. Suddenly she became very happy. Marilla was worried about this sudden change.

As soon as Anne saw Mrs Rachel, she knelt• at Mrs Rachel's feet.

'Oh, Mrs Rachel, I am so very sorry,' said Anne. 'I behaved terribly. I disgraced Matthew and Marilla. It was very bad of me to get so angry because you told the truth. What I said to you was also true. But I was wrong to say it. Oh, Mrs Rachel, please forgive me.'

Anne waited for Mrs Rachel's response.

Anne was very sincere•. But Marilla saw that Anne was enjoying her apology. This was not right for a punishment.

Fortunately, Mrs Rachel didn't notice Anne's enjoyment.

Mrs Rachel forgave Anne immediately.

'Stand up, child,' said Mrs Rachel. 'I forgive you. I was a little too honest. But I do tell the truth. Don't take my words seriously. It's true that your hair is very red. But hair can get darker.'

'Oh, Mrs Rachel,' Anne stood. 'Oh, imagining my hair darker is so wonderful. Now can I go to your garden? I can imagine better out there.'

'Oh, yes. And you can pick some white flowers.'

Anne went outside.

'She's strange but there's something nice about her,' said Mrs Rachel. 'I understand why you kept her now. She does need training. A child with a quick temper probably isn't dishonest. I think I like her.'

Glossary

- **knelt:** got on to the floor on her knees
- **mood:** emotional state
- **sincere:** honest

Marilla and Anne walked home. It was getting dark.

'Do you think I apologized well?' asked Anne.

'You did apologize well,' said Marilla. She wanted to laugh at the memory. 'I hope you don't need to make many more apologies. You need to control your temper, Anne.'

'That isn't so hard. But I'm *so* tired of being teased• about my hair,' said Anne. 'It makes me really angry. I love pretty things. And I hate looking in a mirror and seeing something that isn't pretty. Oh, I feel good about Mrs Rachel now. It's a lovely feeling to apologize and to be forgiven.'

'Anne, be quiet,' said Marilla. She was tired of Anne's chatter•. Anne was quiet for a while. Then she suddenly held Marilla's hand.

'I love Green Gables already,' said Anne. 'No place seemed like home before. Oh, Marilla, I'm so happy.'

Marilla felt very good. Anne's hand gave her a warm feeling. Maybe like a mother's feeling. Quickly she thought of a moral to tell Anne.

'You can always be happy by being good. And by saying your prayers.'

'I'm going to imagine some prayers now. So I'm not going to talk any more right now, Marilla.'

'Good,' said Marilla.

MARILLA
How does Anne make Marilla laugh and feel good?
Write a list.

chatter: constant talking

teased: laughed at

10 Anne meets her best friend

It was a Sunday morning. Anne was in her bedroom looking at three new dresses on the bed. There was a brown dress, a black-and-white one and an ugly blue one.

Marilla made the dresses. All three were very simple.

'Anne, do you like your new dresses?' asked Marilla.

'I can *imagine* that I like them,' said Anne sadly.

'Oh, I can see that you don't like the dresses. But they are new. Why don't you like them?'

'They're… they're not… pretty,' said Anne.

'You are vain•, Anne,' said Marilla. 'They are sensible dresses. The blue and the brown dresses can be for school. The black-and-white one can be for church and Sunday school•. You must be grateful• to have new dresses.'

'Oh, I am grateful,' said Anne. 'But I really wanted a white dress with puffy sleeves•. I prayed for one.'

'You do say ridiculous• things,' said Marilla. 'Now put on the black-and-white one for Sunday school and come downstairs.'

CLOTHES

What do you like wearing?
Are clothes important for you?
Tell a friend.

- **grateful:** full of thanks; happy
- **puffy sleeves:**

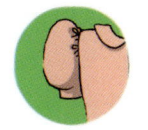

- **ridiculous:** strange and stupid
- **Sunday school:** a class at church on a Sunday where you learn about Jesus
- **vain:** obsessed with how you look

Anne wore the black-and-white dress and a hat but she felt very plain. As she was walking to Sunday school she saw some roses. She picked them and put them in her hat. This made her feel prettier.

But no one at Sunday school was very friendly. All the other little girls thought Anne was strange with roses in her hat.

'Well, how was Sunday school?' asked Marilla, when Anne got home.

'I didn't like it. It was horrible. I behaved well. No one talked to me. There were nine girls. They all had puffy sleeves.'

'You can't think about your sleeves at Sunday school. You need to listen to the lesson.'

'Oh, but I answered a lot of questions. Then we went into the church and the sermon• was very long. So I daydreamed.'

'Anne,' said Marilla 'I want you to be good. But listen, I have some news for you. Diana Barry came home this afternoon. We can go meet Diana together.'

'Oh, Marilla, I'm frightened. Oh, I hope she doesn't hate me. Oh, how tragic!'

'Now, don't worry. Diana is going to like you. But Mrs Barry chooses Diana's friends. So you must be very polite. And don't say anything silly•.'

Anne was trembling•. She was excited to meet Diana, but she was also afraid of Mrs Barry.

Anne and Marilla walked to Mrs Barry's house. Mrs Barry answered the door. She was a tall woman. People said she was very strict with her children.

Glossary

- **sermon:** talk on a religious or moral subject, usually in a church
- **silly:** stupid; foolish
- **trembling:** when your body is moving quickly because you are afraid

'How do you do, Marilla?' said Mrs Barry politely. 'Come in. And is this your adopted girl?'

'Yes, this is Anne Shirley,' said Marilla.

'Spelled with an E,' said Anne.

Mrs Barry didn't respond. She shook hands. Then she said kindly: 'How are you?'

'I am well in body but considerably• disturbed• in spirit, thank you,' Anne said seriously.

INTRODUCTIONS

What does Anne say? Is it silly?
Match.

a) How do you do?   1 ☐ I'm fine.
b) How are you?   2 ☐ I'm eleven.
c) How old are you?   3 ☐ Nice to meet you.

Diana was sitting on the sofa. She was reading. She was a very pretty girl. She had her mother's black eyes and hair and a very happy face.

'This is my daughter Diana,' said Mrs Barry. 'Diana, take Anne outside into the garden to play.'

The girls went outside.

'Diana reads too much,' said Mrs Barry to Marilla. 'I can't stop her. She needs to play with a friend.'

Glossary

- **considerably:** (here) very
- **disturbed:** (here) not serene or peaceful
- **swear:** promise something very seriously

Anne and Diana stood in the garden. They were looking at each other shyly.

The Barry garden was beautiful.

'Oh, Diana,' said Anne. 'Do you think you can like me enough to be my best friend?'

'I think so,' said Diana. 'I'm very glad you came to Green Gables. It's great to have somebody to play with.'

'Do you swear• to be my friend forever and ever?' asked Anne.

Diana nodded her head and the girls swore to be friends forever.

'You're a strange girl, Anne,' said Diana. 'But I'm going to like you a lot.'

'Well, do you think Diana can be a best friend?' asked Marilla when they were back at Green Gables.

'Oh yes,' said Anne. 'Oh Marilla, I'm so happy. Diana's going to give me a picture to put up in my room. I wish I had something to give Diana.'

'Well, remember you're not going to play all the time,' said Marilla. 'You have work to do, too.'

Anne was so happy, she had a best friend now.

Later Matthew gave Anne a box of chocolates.

'Chocolates are bad for her,' said Marilla. 'Anne, don't look so sad. You can eat them. But don't eat all of them at once•.'

'Oh, no, certainly not,' said Anne happily. 'I can eat one tonight, Marilla. And I can give Diana half of them. It's wonderful that I have something to give Diana.'

Anne went to her bedroom.

'Well, she isn't mean,' said Marilla. 'I'm glad. Now, don't laugh Matthew but do you know something? I can't imagine Green Gables without Anne.'

IMAGINE

Is there someone you can't imagine life without?
Tell a friend.
I can't imagine life without...

• **at once:** at the same time; together

11 The picnic

It was a hot August afternoon.

'Oh, Marilla, there's going to be a Sunday school picnic next week. And someone is going to make ice cream. Marilla, *ice cream*. Can I go?'

'Anne. What time did I tell you to come in•?'

'Two o'clock. But isn't it wonderful about the picnic, Marilla? Please can I go? I dreamed of picnics, but I never...'

'Yes, I told you to come at two o'clock. It's a quarter to three. Why didn't you obey• me, Anne?'

'I wanted to, Marilla, I really did. But I went to tell Matthew about the picnic before coming in. Please can I go?'

'You must learn to obey my orders. As for the picnic, of course you can go. All the other girls from Sunday school are going, aren't they?'

'Yes, but...' said Anne. She was worried. 'I must take some food. I can't cook, Marilla. I can go to a picnic without puffy sleeves. But I can't go without food. I am very worried.'

'Well, stop worrying. I can cook something.'

'Oh Marilla, you are so kind to me. I'm so grateful for everything.'

Anne ran into Marilla's arms and kissed Marilla's cheek.

'Stop that kissing nonsense,' said Marilla. 'I'm going to teach you to cook one day. But I am waiting for you to be more serious. You can't daydream with cooking. Now, sit down and do your patchwork•.'

- **come in:** come back home
- **obey:** do what she said
- **patchwork:** lots of different squares of material sewn together

'I do *not* like patchwork,' said Anne. But she sat down and started. 'I think some sewing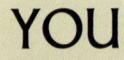 is nice but I wish time went quickly like it does when I'm playing with Diana. We have great fun, Marilla. I have to provide most of the imagination. Diana is perfect in every other way. Oh, I hope it's sunny next Wednesday for the picnic. Ice cream!'

'Anne, can you please stop talking for ten minutes,' said Marilla with a smile.'

Anne was silent for ten minutes.

But she talked about the picnic for the rest of the week.

On Sunday Anne and Marilla were coming home from church.

'The minister talked about the picnic and I really felt excited,' said Anne.

'You get too excited about things, Anne,' said Marilla. 'You are going to have many disappointments in your life.'

'Oh, Marilla, looking forward to things is nice,' said Anne. 'I think it is worse to not look forward to anything than to be disappointed.'

YOU
What do you 'look forward to' every week? Tell a friend.

 Glossary

- **amethyst brooch:**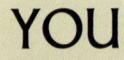
- **disappointments:** when things happen differently and make you sad
- **sewing:**

Marilla wore her amethyst brooch● to church that Sunday. The brooch was Marilla's favorite possession. It had a border of tiny amethysts. It was special to Marilla because it was from her mother. Anne saw and admired the brooch.

'Oh, Marilla, it's a very elegant brooch. I don't know how you can concentrate in church with the brooch right here. Can I hold the brooch for one minute? '

Then on Monday evening before the picnic Marilla was looking for her brooch.

'Do you know where my amethyst brooch is? I can't find it anywhere.'

'I was passing your bedroom this afternoon,' said Anne, slowly. 'I saw the brooch. Then I put it on for one minute to see how it looked.'

'Anne don't ever go into my bedroom without an invitation. Where did you leave it?'

'I left it on the table. I'm sorry, Marilla. I promise never to do it again. I never do the same naughty thing again.'

Marilla looked everywhere. But she couldn't find the brooch.

'Anne, the brooch is gone. Did you lose it?'

Anne looked directly at Marilla. 'No, I didn't take the brooch from your room.'

'You are lying●, Anne,' said Marilla, angrily. 'Go to your room until you are ready to confess●.'

Anne went to her bedroom.

'She is probably worried about punishment. I am disappointed,' thought Marilla. 'I don't like lying.'

Marilla told Matthew the story the next morning. He didn't believe that Anne lied. But the story was strange.

'Did the brooch fall somewhere?' asked Matthew.

'I looked everywhere in my bedroom,' said Marilla. 'The brooch is gone. Anne took it and she told me a lie.'

'What are you going to do?' Matthew asked.

'She can stay in her room until she confesses,' said Marilla. 'Then she must be severely punished.'

'Yes, you have to punish her,' said Matthew.

LYING

Do you think Anne is lying or telling the truth? Why?

Discuss in groups.

 **Glossary**

● **confess:** when you say you did something bad

lying: saying something that is not true

Marilla went to speak to Anne again.

'You can stay in this room until you confess,' said Marilla.

'But the picnic is tomorrow, Marilla,' cried Anne. 'I promise to stay here as long as you like *after* the picnic.'

'You are not going to the picnic until you confess.'

Wednesday morning arrived. It was the day of the picnic. It was a perfect day. Anne was sitting very still on her bed. Marilla entered Anne's bedroom.

'Marilla, I'm ready to confess.'

'Well, tell me,' said Marilla.

'I took the brooch,' said Anne. She spoke mechanically. 'I took it because I wanted to play with it. I wanted to imagine I was a lady with an expensive brooch. I took it outside. Then, when I was walking over the bridge by the lake the brooch fell from my hand. It sank to the bottom of the lake. And that's my best confession, Marilla.'

Marilla was angry. Anne lost the brooch and didn't feel guilty•.

'Anne, this is terrible,' Marilla said. 'You are very naughty.'

'Yes. I know I have to be punished,' agreed Anne calmly. 'Please do it now. I want to go to the picnic without guilt.'

'You are not going to the picnic. That is your punishment.'

'What?' Anne stood suddenly. 'Oh, Marilla, that was why I confessed. Any punishment except that. Oh, Marilla, please, can I go to the picnic? Please.'

'You are not going to the picnic.'

Anne threw her body on the bed and cried.

Marilla left the room quickly. 'Oh dear, Mrs Rachel was right. But I began this work with Anne. I must continue.'

At lunch-time Marilla called Anne.

'Come and have lunch, Anne.'

'I can't eat anything,' said Anne. 'My heart is broken.'

Marilla was very annoyed•. She spoke to Matthew.

'Well, she wasn't right taking the brooch. And telling lies was bad,' said Matthew. 'But she's so young. I think she needs to go to that picnic.'

'Matthew, I think I was too easy with her. And she doesn't understand that she was naughty. You're defending her.'

Matthew was quiet. He didn't agree with Marilla.

After lunch Marilla remembered she had to repair• her shawl•.

The shawl was in a box on the table in her room. Marilla lifted it. It seemed that something was attached to the shawl. It glittered•. It was the amethyst brooch.

'Oh dear,' said Marilla, 'Here's my brooch. But Anne said she took it and lost it.'

Glossary

- **annoyed:** angry
- **glittered:** sparkled with bits of light
- **guilty:** responsible or bad
- **repair:** make something good again
- **shawl:** a piece of material women wear on their shoulders

Marilla went to Anne's bedroom with the brooch.

'Anne,' said Marilla. 'I found my brooch attached to my shawl. Why did you invent that story this morning?'

'Well, you said I must stay in my bedroom until I confessed,' said Anne, 'So I invented a story. But then you said I wasn't going to the picnic. So my work was wasted•.'

'Anne, that is ridiculous,' said Marilla. 'I was wrong. I made you confess. Please forgive me, Anne. I can forgive you and we can start again. And now get ready for that picnic.'

That night after the picnic, a very happy Anne returned to Green Gables.

'Oh, Marilla, everything was lovely today. We had a wonderful tea. Then we went in a boat on the lake. And we had ice cream. Oh Marilla, it was superb•.'

Later when Anne was in bed, Marilla went to talk to Matthew.

'I made a mistake and I learned a lesson,' said Marilla. 'Anne is different. But I believe she is going to be alright. And life is never boring with Anne around.'

DIFFERENT
How is Anne different?
Do you think it is good to be different? Why?/Why not?
Discuss in small groups.

Glossary

• **superb:** wonderful
• **wasted:** not necessary

12 Anne starts school

It was September and Anne started school with Diana. Marilla was worried about Anne starting school. But Anne came home very happy after her first day.

'I think I'm going to like school,' said Anne. 'The teacher's name is Mr Philips. But I don't like him very much.'

'Anne Shirley,' said Marilla. 'You don't go to school to criticize the teacher. Your job is to learn. I hope you behaved.'

'I did,' said Anne. 'There are lots of nice girls in school. I'm not as good as the others. They're all on the Grade 5 book. I'm only on the Grade 4 book. I feel a little ashamed. But there's nobody with my imagination.'

Three weeks later, Anne and Diana were walking happily to school together.

'I think Gilbert Blythe is coming back to school today,' said Diana. 'He was away visiting his cousins. He's *very* handsome. And he teases the girls a lot.'

Anne didn't know much about Gilbert.

'Gilbert is in our class,' said Diana. 'He's only on the Grade 4 book but he's almost fourteen. You're going to have some competition with Gilbert.'

'I'm glad,' said Anne. 'I can't really be proud of being the best of the younger boys and girls.

SCHOOL
When does your school start each year?

Later in the classroom Diana whispered to Anne, 'That's Gilbert Blythe over there. Do you think he's handsome?'

Anne looked. Gilbert Blythe was tying Ruby Gillis' hair to the seat. He was handsome. Suddenly Ruby Gillis tried to stand. She screamed. Everybody looked. Mr Phillips looked angrily at Ruby. Gilbert pretended he was innocent. Then he looked at Anne and winked• at her.

'I think Gilbert Blythe *is* handsome,' said Anne. 'But winking at a stranger isn't polite.'

Later in the afternoon Mr Phillips was explaining something to Ruby Gillis. The other students were playing. Gilbert Blythe was trying to get Anne's attention. Anne was daydreaming.

Suddenly, Gilbert grabbed• Anne's red hair and whispered: 'Carrots! Carrots!'

Anne was furious.

'You mean, terrible boy!' she said angrily.

Then Anne hit Gilbert on the head with her slate•. The slate broke in half.

'Anne, what are you doing?' said Mr Phillips. Anne didn't answer.

Then Gilbert spoke, 'It was my fault Mr Phillips. I teased her.'

Mr Phillips ignored Gilbert.

'You have a terrible temper, Anne,' said Mr Phillips. 'Stand in front of the blackboard, and you can stay there all afternoon.'

Anne was mortified•. She obeyed Mr Phillips.

Then Mr Phillips wrote:

'Ann Shirley has a very bad temper. Ann Shirley must learn to control her temper.'

Glossary

- **grabbed:** took quickly with force
- **mortified:** very embarrassed
- **slate:** piece of flat black stone that children used to write on at school
- **winked:** closed and opened one eye quickly

ORDER

Put the following events in the correct order.

☐ Mr Phillips spells Anne's name without an E.

☐ Gilbert winks at Anne.

☐ Anne hits Gilbert on the head.

☐ Gilbert grabs Anne's hair and shouts, 'Carrots!'.

☐ Anne has to stand in front of the blackboard.

When school finished Anne left proudly. She was too angry to cry. She was never speaking to Gilbert Blythe *ever* again.

Gilbert tried to apologize. Anne ignored him.

'Oh you must forgive Gilbert, Anne,' said Diana.

'I can't,' said Anne. 'And Mr Phillips spelled my name without an E.'

'You mustn't worry about Gilbert teasing you,' said Diana. 'He teases all the girls. But he never apologized before.'

'Gilbert Blythe hurt my feelings *terribly*, Diana,' said Anne.

The next day Mr Phillips warned• the class not to be late after lunch. 'Late students are going to be punished,' he said.

After lunch Anne ran into the classroom while Mr Phillips was hanging up his hat. The boys arrived a few seconds later.

Mr Phillips was too lazy to punish everyone. He found a scapegoat•.

'Anne Shirley, you were late. As a punishment you can sit with the boys. Sit beside Gilbert Blythe,' he said.

The other boys laughed. Anne stared at Mr Phillips.

She hesitated•. Then she sat beside Gilbert Blythe.

Sitting with a boy was terrible. But sitting next to Gilbert was the worst punishment. She felt angry and humiliated.

FAIR OR UNFAIR?

Was Mr Philips fair to Anne?

Discuss in small groups.

Glossary

- **hesitated:** stopped
- **removed:** took away
- **scapegoat:** person who is punished for the mistakes of others
- **warned:** told in advance of a possible bad situation

When school was finished Anne went to her own desk. She removed• everything.

As they were walking home Anne told Diana she was never going to school again. Then later she told Marilla the same thing.

Marilla saw that Anne did not want to change her mind so she decided to go to Mrs Rachel's house and ask for advice.

'I think she can stay home,' said Mrs Rachel. 'I think that Mr Phillips was wrong. The boys weren't punished. That was unfair.'

'Really?' said Marilla.

'Yes. Wait a week. Then send her back.'

Marilla took Mrs Rachel's advice. Anne studied at home and did her chores. On the weekend she played with Diana.

13 Diana is invited to tea

Marilla was going to a meeting and Anne was allowed to invite Diana for tea. Marilla suggested some special food. There was some raspberry cordial•, too. Marilla told Anne the cordial was on the second shelf• of the sitting-room cupboard•. Anne was really excited about the raspberry cordial.

Diana came over• dressed in her second-best dress. Usually she ran into Anne's kitchen, but today she knocked at the front door.

The two girls chatted like grown-ups• for a few minutes inside. Then they forgot to be dignified and they went outside to play. Diana also had so much to tell Anne about school. Diana said that everybody missed Anne. They wished she was at school again.

At last it was time to have the raspberry cordial. Anne looked on the second shelf of the cupboard but there was nothing there. She found it on the top shelf.

Politely Anne offered Diana some cordial on the veranda. She went into the kitchen to prepare the food. Diana sat drinking the cordial.

When Anne came back from the kitchen, Diana was drinking her third glass of cordial.

'This cordial is so much nicer than Mrs Rachel's,' said Diana.

'Yes, Marilla is a great cook,' said Anne. Then she added, 'Diana are you alright?'

'I suddenly feel very sick,' she said 'I have to go home.'

'Oh, Diana, are you really sick?' said Anne. 'Wait for your tea.'

'I must go home,' repeated Diana. 'I am very dizzy•.'

Anne walked Diana halfway home. She was very disappointed.

Glossary

- **came over:** arrived
- **cordial:** sweet drink made with water, sugar and fruit
- **cupboard:** place where you keep things
- **dizzy:** when your head feels like it's moving in circles
- **grown-ups:** adults
- **shelf:** level

The next day Anne stayed at home all day. On Monday afternoon Anne went to Mrs Rachel's on an errand● but she came home again quickly.

'What's wrong, Anne?' asked Marilla. 'Were you rude to Mrs Rachel again?'

Anne was crying.

'Anne Shirley, tell me why you are crying,' said Marilla.

'Mrs Rachel said that Mrs Barry was very angry,' said Anne. 'Mrs Barry said that I got Diana *drunk*● on Saturday. I am never going to be able to play with Diana again.'

'Anne what did you give Diana to drink?' asked Marilla.

'I gave her raspberry cordial,' cried Anne. 'Three glasses of cordial doesn't make you drunk.'

'Drunk, nonsense!' Marilla opened the cupboard. There was a bottle of currant wine● on the shelf.

'Anne, you gave Diana currant wine and not raspberry cordial. Didn't you know the difference?'

'I didn't taste● it,' said Anne. 'I wanted to be polite. Then Diana got very sick. Mrs Barry doesn't believe that I didn't do it on purpose●.'

'I think Diana was very greedy,' said Marilla. 'Three glasses of any drink can make anyone sick.'

COLOR
What color is raspberry cordial?
What color is currant wine?

Glossary

- **drunk:** after your drink too much alcohol and your head hurts
- **errand:** when you go on a mission to do something
- **farewell:** goodbye forever
- **on purpose:** consciously
- **taste:** try
- **wine:** alcoholic drink made from fruit

'Oh, don't cry,' said Marilla. 'It's not your fault but I'm sorry it happened.'

'Diana and I are separated forever,' said Anne sadly.

Marilla went to speak to Mrs Barry and explain the situation. But Mrs Barry didn't believe Marilla.

So Anne went to see Mrs Barry. But Mrs Barry didn't believe Anne, either.

Mrs Barry made a decision: Anne and Diana were no longer able to be friends.

And that was final.

The next day Diana was allowed to come to Green Gables to explain Mrs Barry's decision.

'Oh Anne,' said Diana with tears in her eyes. 'Mother says I can never play with you again. I'm here to say goodbye. I can only stay ten minutes. She's counting the minutes.'

'Ten minutes isn't very long to say an eternal farewell•,' said Anne. She was crying, too, now. 'Oh, Diana, promise never to forget me. Promise even when you meet dearer friends.'

Anne watched her friend leave. It was sad and romantic.

'It's all over,' Anne informed Marilla later. 'It's worse to lose a friend than not to have one. Diana gave me some of her hair. I'm going to put it in a little bag. If I die, please leave the bag with me. I don't think I am going to live very long, Marilla.'

'I don't think you are going to die, Anne,' said Marilla. She was not sympathetic.

SEPARATION
Imagine you are separated from your best friend. How do you feel?

The following morning Anne surprised Marilla. She was dressed to go to school.

Anne was welcomed back to school. Everyone was happy to see her.

Diana sat next to Gertie Pye and did not look at Anne at all.

'Diana did not even smile at me,' said Anne to Marilla that night. But the next morning at school Anne received a parcel*.

Dear Anne,

Mother says I can't play with you or talk to you even at school. Remember I love you lots. I miss telling you my secrets. I don't like Gertie Pye. I made you a bookmark* from some paper. When you look at it remember me.

Your true friend,

Diana Barry

Anne read the note and kissed the bookmark. She replied.

My darling Diana,

Of course you have to obey your mother. Our spirits can speak. I am going to keep your present forever. Minnie Andrews is a very nice girl. But she has no imagination. She can't be my friend.

Yours until death,

Anne or Cordelia Shirley.

Glossary

- **bookmark:** piece of card to show your place in a book
- **parcel:** package

14 Anne saves a life

It was a cold January evening. Marilla and Mrs Rachel were at Charlottetown, where the Canadian Premier• was speaking.

Meanwhile, Anne and Matthew were in the kitchen at Green Gables. Matthew was reading. Anne was studying.

Anne started talking. She talked and talked. Matthew listened attentively, replying occasionally when necessary.

Suddenly Diana Barry entered the kitchen.

'What's wrong, Diana?' asked Anne.

'Come quickly, Anne,' said Diana. 'Minnie May has croup•. All the adults are in Charlottetown listening to the Premier. Nobody knows what to do. I'm so scared.'

Matthew went outside.

'He went to get the horse. He's going to get the doctor,' said Anne. 'I can read Matthew's thoughts.'

'The doctor is in Charlottetown too, listening to the Premier,' cried Diana. 'Charlottetown is so far away.'

'Don't cry, Diana,' said Anne. '*I* know what to do. You forget that Mrs Hammond had twins three times. They all had croup. Let's go!'

The two girls ran all the way. Anne enjoyed the adventure with her old friend. But she was worried about Minnie May, too.

Minnie May was Diana's little sister. She was only three years old. She had a fever• and she was breathing very loudly.

Anne started working calmly. She gave Minnie May the medicine. Minnie didn't like it. But Anne looked after her all night, giving her the medicine.

Glossary

- **croup:** illness that children get and it's difficult for them to breathe
- **fever:** when your body is too hot and you are very ill
- **Premier:** head of a country or government

Matthew arrived at three o'clock with the doctor. Minnie May was much better and she was sleeping soundly.

Anne spoke to the doctor and he listened to her in amazement.

Later the doctor spoke to Mr and Mrs Barry.

'That redheaded girl from Green Gables saved Minnie May's life. She was clever and calm. There aren't many girls of her age able to save a life like that.'

So of course, Mrs Barry thought about Anne and she felt sorry about her reaction to Diana and the currant wine. She immediately invited Anne for tea. She wanted to apologize and ask Anne to be friends with Diana again.

Later that evening when Anne was back home, she told Marilla and Matthew about her visit to see Mrs Barry.

'Mrs Barry kissed me and apologized,' Anne told them. 'I was very polite and forgave her straight away. We had an elegant tea. Mrs Barry used the best tea set. I felt special. Diana and I had a lovely time playing together. I have red hair but I am so happy.'

After Reading

Personal Response

1 Read each sentence. Which number is most true for you? Circle the number.

> **1 = Not really   5 = Definitely**

a) I like the story.
   1   2   3   4   5
b) The story is easy to understand.
   1   2   3   4   5
c) The story teaches me new words and new expressions.
   1   2   3   4   5
d) I think the story is for people of my age.
   1   2   3   4   5
e) I want to tell a friend to read this story.
   1   2   3   4   5

2 What do you like about the story?

3 Do you think Anne changed in the story? What was she like at the start? What is she like now?

4 What are the messages in the story? Tick (✓).

☐ It is important to know the difference between imagination and reality.

☐ It is good to belong.

☐ It is important to have puffy sleeves.

☐ It is important to forgive.

5 Do you agree with these messages?

After Reading

Comprehension

1 Are the following sentences true (T) or false (F)? Tick (✓).

	T	F
a) Anne had lots of brothers and sisters.	☐	☐
b) Marilla and Matthew are married.	☐	☐
c) Matthew wasn't a handsome man.	☐	☐
d) Anne came to Green Gables because of a mistake.	☐	☐
e) Marilla was a bad woman.	☐	☐
f) Anne didn't have a good imagination.	☐	☐
g) Anne didn't like Mrs Rachel Lynde because she was fat.	☐	☐
h) Diana and Anne had no time to play together.	☐	☐
i) Matthew was very strict with Anne.	☐	☐
j) Gilbert Blythe liked teasing girls.	☐	☐
k) Marilla disliked people who told lies.	☐	☐
l) Anne loved the dresses that Marilla made.	☐	☐
m) Mrs Barry didn't like Anne because she was ugly.	☐	☐
n) Anne knew about sick babies because she was a nurse.	☐	☐

2 Correct the false sentences in Exercise 1.

3 Match the following sentence halves to make a sentence.

a) ☐ The story is set
b) ☐ Marilla and Matthew ask for a child to
c) ☐ Anne asks Diana to swear
d) ☐ Anne loves going to school
e) ☐ Anne thinks sitting with a boy
f) ☐ Anne can imagine

1 but she doesn't like Mr Philips.
2 that she likes her new dresses.
3 to be her friend forever.
4 help them with work around their house and garden.
5 is the worst punishment.
6 in a small town called Avonlea.

4 Which sentences from Exercise 3 match these pictures?

5 Choose the correct answer. Tick (✓).

a) Which description does NOT refer to Anne?

1 ☐ red hair   2 ☐ glasses   3 ☐ freckles

b) What does Anne learn from the episode about the amethyst brooch?

1 ☐ A good imagination is not always useful.
2 ☐ A good imagination is often useful.
3 ☐ A good imagination is always useful.

After Reading

Characters

1 **Match the descriptions to the characters. Write the letters beside the pictures.**

 Anne
 Diana
 Marilla

 Gilbert
 Mrs Rachel Lynde
 Matthew

a) Tall and thin. Dark hair in a bun. Soft mouth.

b) Plaits. Grey eyes. Freckles.

c) Quiet. Sixty years old. Enjoys being alone.

d) Very handsome. Fourteen years old. Sometimes teases girls.

e) Black eyes and black hair. Eleven years old.

f) Fat. Very curious. Helpful.

2 **Match the adjectives to the characters below.**

a) Diana	**1** dizzy
b) Gilbert	**2** mean
c) Marilla	**3** surprised
d) Matthew	**4** handsome
e) Mrs Blewett	**5** nervous

3 Can you find pictures in the book that show the characters as they are described in Exercise 2? Work with a partner. See who can find the matching picture first!

4 What do the characters do? Order the facts below.

a) ☐ Marilla and Matthew ask for a boy.

b) ☐ Marilla discovers that Anne is lying.

c) ☐ Marilla tells Anne she can't go to the picnic.

d) ☐ Marilla finds her brooch.

e) ☐ Marilla tells Anne she can live with them.

f) ☐ Diana and Anne meet.

g) ☐ Anne arrives at the station.

h) ☐ Anne apologizes to Mrs Rachel.

i) ☐ Anne gets three new dresses.

j) ☐ Anne goes to the picnic.

k) ☐ Anne saves Diana's little sister.

l) ☐ Gilbert teases Anne about her hair.

m) ☐ Mr Phillips punishes Anne.

n) ☐ Mrs Barry is angry with Anne.

5 Choose one of the facts above. How do the characters feel? Work with a partner. Write three sentences about what you remember.

Anne is angry with Gilbert because…

Anne doesn't like the dresses because…

After Reading

Plot and Theme

1 **These words are important themes in the story. Match each word to the episode.**

a) belonging   **1** Anne tells a story about how she lost the brooch.

b) telling the truth   **2** Anne wants to live with Marilla and Matthew.

c) imagination   **3** Mrs Rachel accepts Anne's apology.

d) helping people   **4** Anne looks after Minnie May.

e) forgiveness   **5** Anne wants a dress with puffy sleeves.

f) vanity   **6** Anne says she didn't take the brooch.

2 **Look at the pictures and write the correct theme from Exercise 1.**

A .... **B** .... **C** ....

3 **Use the following words to complete the sentences.**

> orphanage   alone   belonged to   pretty

a) Anne's childhood was very sad until she .... Marilla and Matthew.

b) Anne was living in an .... because her parents died.

c) Anne didn't have any living relations, she was completely ...., so she lived in an orphanage.

d) Anne loved .... clothes. She wanted a dress with puffy sleeves and she prayed for one.

K 4 **There are lots of conversations in the book. Match the question with the best response.**

a) ☐ 'Good evening, Rachel. How is your family?'

1 'Is that your name?'

b) ☐ 'I'm sorry I was late. Give me your bag.'

2 'I am well, thank you.'

c) ☐ 'Can you please call me Cordelia?'

3 'We're all quite well.'

d) ☐ 'Can I call you Aunt Marilla?'

4 'No, just call me Marilla.'

e) ☐ 'How are you?'

5 'Oh, I can carry it.'

K 5 **Use the <u>questions</u> above to start a conversation. Work with a partner. Try to speak for 1 minute.**

6 **Match this picture to one of the conversations in Exercise 4.**

7 **Use the following words to complete the text about Anne's friends.**

> great   best   imaginary   real   important   imaginary

Friends are **a)** .... to Anne. When she lives with Mrs Thomas, Anne has an **b)** .... friend. She calls her Katie Maurice. She tells her everything. When she lives with Mrs Hammond she has another **c)** .... friend. Her name is Violetta. They are **d)** .... friends. At Green Gables Marilla wants Anne to have a **e)** .... friend. Marilla helps Anne to meet Diana. Anne and Diana become **f)** .... friends and swear to be friends forever.

After Reading

Language

1 **Complete the sentences with these words from the story.**

> plates   slate   horse and buggy   desks   brooch   shawl

a) He rode the ....
to the station.

b) All the children had to be at their .... before
the start of the lesson.

c) She wore an old .... on her shoulders because
it was cold.

d) The table was set for supper. There were three ....
on the table.

e) Her .... was from her mother and it was her
favorite possession.

f) Anne hit Gilbert on the head with her ....

2 **Past simple or past continuous? Put the verb in brackets in the correct form.**

a) It was a cold January evening. Marilla and Mrs Rachel were at
Charlottetown, where the Canadian Premier ....
(speak).

b) Meanwhile, Anne and Matthew were in the kitchen at Green
Gables. Matthew .... (read). Anne ....
(study).

c) Anne started talking. She .... (talk) and talked.

d) Suddenly Diana Barry .... (enter) the kitchen.

e) All the adults .... (be) in Charlottetown listening
to the Premier.

K **3** **Complete the letter. Use the words below.**

know you ask be buy for like tell polite to

Dear Diana,
How are (a)................? I want to invite you to come
(b)................ my house. Can you come for tea on Saturday? Please
(c)................ your mother. I hope she agrees.
We are going to (d)................ some very special things. I know it's
not (e)................ to say what you're going to have, but I have to
(f)................ you that we are having cordial!
I am excited to have you here (g)................ tea. Is there some food
that you would (h)................? Please tell me. I want this tea to
(i)................ very special.
Let me (j)................ about Saturday!
Bye for now,
        Anne or Cordelia Shirley.

4 **Complete the sentences below with *and*, *so*, *but* or *because*.**

a) Then he looked at Anne .... winked at her.

b) 'You don't want me .... I'm not a boy.

c) 'Now, I know you like talking, ... tell me about your life.'

d) She had twins three times. I like babies, ... twins three times is too much.

5 **Circle the best word.**

a) 'Did you go to school?' *said/asked* Marilla.

b) Marilla *said/asked* no more questions.

c) 'Yes. Apologize. That's the word,' said Matthew. '*Say/Tell* it.'

d) But I didn't want to *say/tell* Mrs Rachel. It is so humiliating.

e) 'I can't *apologize/forgive* to Mrs Rachel. I'm not sorry.

f) But I was wrong to say it. Oh, Mrs Rachel, please *apologize/forgive* me.'

After Reading

Exit Test

1 Listen and tick (✓) the correct picture.

a) 1  2

b) 1  2

c) 1  2

d) 1  2

**K 2 Read the sentences about the story.
Choose the best word (1, 2 or 3) for each space.**

a) The story .... when Anne is sent to Prince Edward Island.
1 finishes   **2** begins   **3** ends

b) They decide to adopt a boy .... the orphanage to help Matthew on their farm.
1 from   **2** of   **3** on

c) Marilla thinks Anne talks too .... in the beginning.
1 a lot   **2** many   **3** much

d) The main theme of the story is learning the difference .... imagination and reality.
1 between   **2** among   **3** with

e) Marilla and Matthew Cuthbert are ....
1 husband and wife   **2** brother and sister
3 mother and father

f) Marilla .... Anne she can stay.
1 tells   **2** says   **3** asks

g) He teases her .... Anne decides to hate him forever.
1 and   **2** but   **3** because

h) Anne promises to be .... at school and home.
1 vain   **2** good   **3** surprised

3 Look at the picture on page 17. Work with a partner. Ask and answer questions about the picture.

Who can you see in the picture?

I can see...

After Reading

Project

Invent a club

1 **Invent a new club. A club is a group of people who like doing the same things.**

a) Work in groups of two or three.

b) Talk about who belongs and who doesn't.

c) Decide on a place to have your club.

d) Now decide on a name for your club.

e) Make a poster about your club. Include the following:

- ✿ *Name* (show why it is called this name)
- ✿ *Where it is*
- ✿ *What you can see there*
- ✿ *Who can go* (eg. 'Teachers are not allowed!')
- ✿ *What you want to do there* (club activities like secret meetings, making jewellery, or building a club house)

f) Present your project to the class. The class can vote for the best club to join.